STEVENSON · WATTERS · NOWAK · LAIHO

LUMBERJANES

A TERRIBLE PLAN

BOOM! BOX

BOOM! BOX™

LUMBERJANES Volume Three, February 2016. Published by BOOM! Box, a division of Boom Entertainment, Inc. Lumberjanes is ™ & © 2016 Shannon Watters, Grace Ellis, Noelle Stevenson & Brooke Allen. Originally published in single magazine form as LUMBERJANES No. 9-12. ™ & © 2015 Shannon Watters, Grace Ellis, Noelle Stevenson & Brooke Allen. All rights reserved. BOOM! Box™ and the BOOM! Box logo are trademarks of Boom Entertainment, Inc., registered in various countries and categories. All characters, events, and institutions depicted herein are fictional. Any similarity between any of the names, characters, persons, events, and/or institutions in this publication to actual names, characters, and persons, whether living or dead, events, and/or institutions is unintended and purely coincidental. BOOM! Box does not read or accept unsolicited submissions of ideas, stories, or artwork.

A catalog record of this book is available from OCLC and from the BOOM! Studios website, www.boom-studios.com, on the Librarians Page.

BOOM! Studios, 5670 Wilshire Boulevard, Suite 450, Los Angeles, CA 90036-5679. Printed in China. First Printing.

ISBN: 978-1-60886-803-2, eISBN: 978-1-61398-474-1

THIS LUMBERJANES FIELD MANUAL BELONGS TO:

NAME:_____

TROOP:_____

DATE INVESTED:_____

FIELD MANUAL TABLE OF CONTENTS

LUMBERJANES
FIELD MANUAL

For the Intermediate Program

Tenth Edition • March 1984

Prepared for the

**Miss Qiunzella Thiskwin
Penniquiqul Thistle Crumpet's**

CAMP FOR ~~GIRLS~~ HARDCORE LADY-TYPES

"Friendship to the Max!"

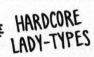

A MESSAGE FROM THE LUMBERJANES HIGH COUNCIL

Catch and release is an essential part of learning how to fish and it also teaches us how to deal with many things that we might come across throughout our long-lived lives. In most cases anglers can keep their catch as a trophy or for their table. This is no different than when you pass a course and get to move forward in your education, you are essentially taking your trophy with you to move to the next step. Some trophies in life might be actual physical trophies but most will not be, they will be something that you will take you with and you with share with others, whether you realize it or not. When it comes to catch and release, there are cases when fish are released by state fishing rules and regulations or by choice. In the case of fishing rules and regulations, the fish may be under-sized, or the species may be regulated, or the waters themselves may be regulated. In other cases, it may be the intent of the angler from the outset. In all cases, every effort should be made to release fish quickly and unharmed. The rules are there for a reason, and just as any young scout will learn as they prepare for their first catch, these rules are meant to keep us safe and everything around us safe.

Rules are important. The rules are there for a reason. Rules give us a way to regulate ourselves, they give us a chance to enter worlds that we once only dreamed of as little girls. Think about the benefits of proper catch and release and how with those rules, it has proven vital to the future of a number of important fisheries around the country as it is a means of preserving and enhancing fish populations. By following the rules anglers contribute to fishing's long-standing commitment to conservation and preservation of our natural resources, a commitment that we share as a Lumberjane.

At this camp we look forward to showing you the world through our eyes, and we look forward to teaching you the practices and rules that will not only make your time with us enjoyable, but also unforgettable.

THE LUMBERJANES PLEDGE

*I solemnly swear to do my best
Every day, and in all that I do,
To be brave and strong,
To be truthful and compassionate,
To be interesting and interested,
To pay attention and question
The world around me,
To think of others first,
To always help and protect my friends,*
~~_____~~
*And to make the world a better place
For Lumberjane scouts
And for everyone else.*

THEN THERE'S A LINE ABOUT GOD, OR WHATEVER

LUMBERJANES™

A TERRIBLE PLAN

Written by

Noelle Stevenson
& Shannon Watters

"If You Got It Haunt It"
Illustrated by
Brittney Williams

"Wrong Number"
Illustrated by
Aimee Fleck

"Ghost Girl"
Written and Illustrated by
Faith Erin Hicks
with colors by **Maarta Laiho**

"Bad Candy"
Illustrated by
Rebecca Tobin

"Lonely Road"
Illustrated by
Carolyn Nowak

"Tailypo"
Illustrated by
Felicia Choo

"Old Betty"
Illustrated by
T. Zysk

Illustrated by

Carolyn Nowak
(Chapters Ten through Twelve)

Colors by

Maarta Laiho
(Chapters Ten through Twelve)

Letters by

Aubrey Aiese

Cover by

Noelle Stevenson

Badge Designs
Kate Leth and Scott Newman

Designer
Scott Newman

Associate Editor
Whitney Leopard

Editor
Dafna Pleban

Special thanks to **Kelsey Pate**
for giving the Lumberjanes their name.

Created by **Shannon Watters, Grace Ellis, Noelle Stevenson & Brooke Allen**

LUMBERJANES FIELD MANUAL
CHAPTER NINE

Lumberjanes "Out-of-Doors" Program Field

IF YOU GOT IT, HAUNT IT BADGE

"Because you weren't going to sleep anyway."

Things go bump in the night, it's basically the best time to go bump if one had to choose a timeframe. This is a lesson that every Lumberjane will learn as she continues on her path. Every Lumberjane should leave camp with the basic understanding of what is out there, how it could get you, and why it won't. She will encounter many problems through life and it will be this knowledge that will help her through. Scary stories are more than just a chance to give your neighbor goosebumps, they are also a chance for you to share your knowledge in a way that is not only fun, but entertaining. After all, aren't the best scary tales the ones that have a little truth to them? It should come as no surprise that both friendship and scary story telling are combined in the *If You Got It, Haunt It* badge.

Haunting is just a fact of life. Spirits are everywhere. Both living and long past, they often want to reach out to

us in the only ways they know how. A Lumberjane will want to not only help these spirits, but with her friends, she'll be able to go above and beyond the call of a scout. And if she is unable to connect with the spirits as so many before her have, well then hopefully she'll at least be able to come up with a good story or two around the camp fire.

To obtain the *If You Got It, Haunt It* badge, a Lumberjane must have already received her *Up All Night* badge, and should have shown great promise in her creative thinking skills. A good picture might be worth a thousand words, but in the same amount of words, a good story is only the beginning. There are many things we can learn from the great storytellers before us. The women who put pen to paper and wove such intricate drama that their stories still stick with us to this very day. It is important for a Lumberjane to

who had a whole bunch of brothers and sisters and great friends and an awesome dog and maybe also a kitty and her life was super good. Every night she'd go to sleep in her own upstairs bedroom and a candy would be sitting on the windowsill just begging her to eat it because candy is delicious and rules.

but she never would though because where is the candy coming from?!

one night she got home and there was the candy and it looked really good, it had a pretty wrapper and smelled like strawberries and chocolate so she ate it.

when she woke up she wasn't in bed anymore... she was in a giant room that looked like evil candy everywhere and she was all wrapped up and trapped in taffy. Staring at her was a lady who had a spider body and a mean smile.

you ate my candy and accepted my contract. now I'm going to eat you.

there's no escape. you're never going to see any of your nice life again!

...and then she was really scared because her family and friends and her dog and her kitty didn't know she was here and she... she was all alone, and she wasn't used to being all alone...

she... she didn't know what to do... noone could come rescue her... she was trapped and alone... her brothers couldn't come scoop her up, her friends couldn't come in and beat up the monster, she didn't know what to do... it's... it's scary being alone......

But it turns out that her fearless dog and cat followed the monster when it took her!

And just at that moment when it seemed hopeless, they jumped in and attacked him!

You're not alone, Rip.

They totally beat him up! He was finished!

Thanks for helping me tell my story, guys!

Okay so there was this lady...

...and she lived alone I guess in a scary castle? Because OF COURSE SHE WOULD, THAT MAKES SO MUCH SENSE, LET'S JUST WILLINGLY PUT OURSELVES IN MORTAL PERIL, WHY NOT and maybe it's a haunted castle? Which I never understood, SELL YOUR HAUNTED CASTLE, who needs the stress--

JEN. NO.

I've got a story.

And it's 100% TRUE.

ONCE, THERE WAS A YOUNG COUPLE, DRIVING HOME AT NIGHT IN THE WINTER. IT WAS ALREADY LATE, SO THE MAN DECIDED TO TAKE A SHORTCUT.

WITHIN MINUTES, OF COURSE, THEY WERE LOST.

BEFORE THEY COULD MANAGE TO FIND THEIR WAY, THEIR TIRE BLEW OUT...

POP!

...SENDING THEM CAREENING INTO A SHALLOW DITCH JUST OFF THE ROAD.

IT WAS MUCH TOO COLD FOR THEM TO WALK ANYWHERE, AND THEY WERE LOST TOO REMOTELY TO CALL FOR HELP. ALL THE COUPLE COULD DO WAS SIT IN THE WARMTH OF THE RUNNING CAR AND WAIT UNTIL MORNING.

THE WOMAN SOON FELL ASLEEP, AND IT WAS THEN THAT THE MAN BEGAN TO HEAR LONG, DISQUIETING SCRATCHES PULLING ALONG THE TOP OF THE CAR.

AT FIRST HE THOUGHT IT WAS THE WIND, BUT THE SCRATCHES CONTINUED TO GET LOUDER...AND LOUDER...

EVENTUALLY IT WAS ALL THE MAN COULD HEAR!! SCRATCHES COMING FROM EVERY DIRECTION, SOMEONE... SOMETHING TRYING TO GET INTO THE CAR, THE SOURCE OBSCURED BY THE THICK SNOW SWIRLING OUTSIDE.

SKRRRR RRRRITCH SKRRRITCHHHH SKRITCHHHH SKRITCH SKRITCHHHH SSSSSSSKRRR

SUDDENLY, WHEN THE MAN FELT HE WOULD SURELY LOSE HIS MIND, CAR LIGHTS CUT THROUGH THE SNOWY DARKNESS OF THE CAR, AND THE SCRATCHING STOPPED.

WAM WAM

IT WAS THE TOWN SHERIFF! SHE YELLED AT THEM TO GET OUT OF THE CAR **NOW** AND COME WITH HER!

THE MAN ROUSED HIS SLEEPY WIFE, BUT COULDN'T RESIST EXAMINING THE CAR AS HE GOT OUT. TO HIS SURPRISE, THERE WAS NOT A BIT OF SNOW DISTURBED! WHERE HAD THOSE NIGHTMARISH SCRATCHING NOISES COME FROM?!

THE MAN GOT INTO THE POLICE CAR AND QUICKLY LAUNCHED INTO HIS TALE. THE SCRATCHING! THE TORMENT! A PSYCHO KILLER ON THE LOOSE! A GHOST!

YOU GUYS HAD A CLOGGED TAILPIPE...

...SAID THE SHERIFF...

CARBON MONOXIDE WAS LEAKING INTO YOUR CAR, CAUSING HALLUCINATIONS. AN HOUR OR SO MORE...

...YOU'D BE **DEAD**.

I'm going to tell the tale of the **TAILYPO**

once, a hermit was making his way through the woods near his cabin. There hadn't been much game that autumn for him & his dog to eat, & he was getting desperate.

Dinner that night was to be some mushrooms & flowers, nothing else.

As they made their way to the blacker part of the forest, suddenly the hermit saw a dark shape...

It was a sleeping animal, huge, unlike any the hermit had ever seen before, with long ears, sharp claws, & a long, thick tail.

Before he could think twice, the hermit brought his hatchet down onto the animal's tail, severing it & sending the creature running deeper into the woods.

triumphant, he & his hound returned to their cabin, making the tail into a delicious stew.

well fed, the man slept soundly for the first time in weeks.

However, something shook him awake soon enough...

Down at the edge of town, surrounded by woods at the edge of a lake, there was a beautiful old house that lay vacant for years and years...

The owner had long vanished, and though it was the envy of every homeowner, no one ever went near it,

because it was rumored to be haunted by the spirit of **Old Betty**, the industrious woman who built the house with her bare hands.

One day, a fellow came to town with intentions of settling down.

It took quite a bit of bribing and refanagling old deeds, but finally, one night, the stranger found himself laying down to sleep on a cot in Old Betty's grandest bedroom, quite satisfied with himself.

He was a prideful man, arrogant, and though he visited every available dwelling in town, he insisted on snatchin' up Old Betty's place.

As he began to fall asleep, however, he heard a quiet hissing sound come off the lake.

Why, someone's in my house but I...

His eyes were suddenly open wide. A musty smell of decay came drifting through the house.

He heard it again, louder, closer.

Why, someone's in my house but I...

Why, someone's in my house but I...

Why, someone's in my house but I...

He heard heavy boots falling on the stairs of the porch, and he pulled the wool of his blanket closer around him as if to attempt to ward it off.

He heard the front door creak open, and he was out of bed, desperately trying a rusted window to escape.

Suddenly the door swung open, and a horrifying voice bellowed...

SOMEONE'S IN MY HOUSE BUT I

A TRESPASSING MAN ATTEMPTING TO FL 24

With one last desperate push, the window was open, and the man was fleeing Old Betty's house, never to be seen in town again.

And Betty? Well, the ruins of her house don't sit too far from here...

and she's still awfully possessive...

No one touch my house but I...

will co...

The...

It help...

appearan...

dress f...

Further...

Lumber...

to have...

part in...

Thiskv...

Hardc...

have...

them...

TELL US A SCARY STORY!

...THE UNIFORM

...should be worn at camp ...events when Lumberjanes ...n may also be worn at other ...ions. It should be worn as a ...the uniform dress with ...rect shoes, and stocking or ...out grows her uniform or ...ng ...ter Lumberjane. ...a she has ...her ...f her

LADIES DIG THE HAT

The...

yellow, short sl...

emb...

the w...

choose...

slacks,...

made o...

out-of-do...

green bere...

the colla...

Shoes ma...

heels, roun...ings or

socks shoul... the shoes or wi...

the uniform. Ne...es, bracelets, or other...elry do...

belong with a Lumberjane uniform.

HOW TO WEAR T...

To look well in a uniform...

uniform be kept in good...

pressed. See that the skirt is the...

height and build, that the belt is a...

that your shoes and stockings are in...the

uniform, that you watch your posture and c...ourself

with dignity and grace. If the beret is removed indoors,

be sure that your hair is neat and kept in place with an

insconspicuous clip or ribbon. When you wear a

Lumberjane uniform you are identified as a member of

this organization and you should be doubly careful to

conduct yourself in a way that will show everyone that

courtesy and thoughtfullness are part of being a

Lumberjane. People are likely to judge a whole nation by

the selfishness of a few individuals, to criticize a whole

family because of the misconduct of one member, and to

feel unkindly toward and organization because of the

The unifor...

helps to cre...

in a group. ...

active life th...

another bond...

future, and pr...

in order to b...

Lumberjane pr...

Penniquiqul Thi... ...ore Lady

Types, but m... ...es will wish to have one. They

can either b... ...e uniform, or make it themselves from

materials available at the trading post.

WELCOME TO SCARE TOWN, POPULATION: YOU

LUMBERJANES FIELD MANUAL
CHAPTER TEN

Lumberjanes "Cooking" Program Field

ABSENCE MAKES THE HEART GROW FONDANT BADGE

"Fondant gives the heart diabetes, it's the circle of life."

Everyone and everything needs food to survive. It is not something that is unique only to people or to creatures and it is something everyone must acknowledge. At Lumberjane camp, every scout will learn that while food is essential, that doesn't mean we can't have some fun with it first. Now while some ladies may have been taught that it is not polite to play with their food, the Lumberjane High Council disagrees. Everything is meant to be fun and exhilarating, we should constantly be learning and improving ourselves just as we should always be laughing. Life is meant to be fun and if that means we get to bake some cakes in the process then every Lumberjane should put on her best apron and go at it.

The *Absence Makes The Heart Grow Fondant* badge represents a skill that all Lumberjanes will be taught. As a Lumberjane it will be understood that every scout should be able to rely on just herself in any situation. That means

she should not only know how to handle a bear attack without harming herself or the animals around her, but she should also know how to create an elaborate cake that will entertain all her guests not only visually but as well as in flavor. The way around the kitchen will be no match for any Lumberjane as she masters her adaptability and her problem solving skills while at this camp.

To obtain the *Absence Makes The Heart Grow Fondant* badge a Lumberjane must be participating in a bake off. She will be given an already baked cake of her choice of flavor as well as the tools to mold her frosting to the design she prefers. Once the time starts the Lumberjane scout must completely decorate her cake in a creative style that will be judged by the leader of the class, and while all art is subjective, the instructions given before the bake off will be clearly given and understood by all participants. In the end, it will be the scout who

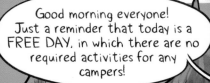
Good morning everyone! Just a reminder that today is a FREE DAY, in which there are no required activities for any campers!

"Remember to bring your own axe if you'll be attending my whittling lessons in Woolpit Lodge, and that all counselors will be leading activities throughout the day. Please check the bulletin board in the mess hall for times and locations.

"I encourage you all to take this as an opportunity to challenge yourself..."

will con...

The out...
It helps...
appearar...
dress fo...
Further...
Lumber...
to have...
part in...
Thiskv...
Hardc...
have...
them...

THE UNIFORM

...should be worn at camp
...events when Lumberjanes
...n may also be worn at other
...ions. It should be worn as a
...the uniform dress with
...rrect shoes, and stocking or

...out grows her uniform or
...ter Lumberjane.
...a she has
...her
...her

WERE WE SCARED? YOU BET JURASSIC!

The...
yellow, short sl...
emb...
the w...
choose...
slacks, ...
made o...
out-of-dc...
green bere...
the colla...
Shoes ma...
heels, rou...
socks shou...
the uniform. Ne...
belong with a Lumberjane uniform.

...GES

NEVER BACK BUBBLES INTO A CORNER

HOW TO WEAR THE UNIFOR...

To look well in a uniform dema...
uniform be kept in good condit...
pressed. See that the skirt is the right...
height and build, that the belt is adjus...
that your shoes and stockings are in k...
uniform, that you watch your posture and...
with dignity and grace. If the beret is remo...
be sure that your hair is neat and kept in pla...with an
insconspicuous clip or ribbon. When you wear a
Lumberjane uniform you are identified as a member of
this organization and you should be doubly careful to
conduct yourself in a way that will show everyone that
courtesy and thoughtfullness are part of being a
Lumberjane. People are likely to judge a whole nation by
the selfishness of a few individuals, to criticize a whole
family because of the misconduct of one member, and to
feel unkindly toward and organization because of the

The unifor...
helps to cre...
in a group. ...
active life th...
another bond...
future, and pr...
in order to b...
Lumberjane pr...
Penniquiqul Thi...
Types, but m...
can either bu...
materials available at the trading post.

APRIL IS WHAT YOU'D CALL AN "INTENSE" READER

...ore Lady
...s will wish to have one. They
...the uniform, or make it themselves from

LUMBERJANES FIELD MANUAL

CHAPTER ELEVEN

Lumberjanes "Arts and Crafts" Program Field

GO BALL-ISTIC BADGE

"Dance like your life depends on it."

There are many things that a Lumberjane will learn while at camp, but one of the camp favorites over these many years has been ballroom dancing. Ballroom dancing is a stress reliever and will teach any Lumberjane scout to put the pressure of the world behind her. The feel and styles of ballroom dances brings the feeling of comfort and great social interaction. Not only that, but it has been shown to help Lumberjanes discover true passion and joy of their life. As a Lumberjanes, she will learn important ballroom dance elements, which include flexibility, superior mental ability, endurance, and strength.

The *Go Ball-istic* badge is not just another step for a Lumberjane on her personal journey in this camp but something much more. Just as many of the other Lumberjane classes will be able to teach and mold the scouts of this camp, it will be ballroom dancing that will show them that not is grace not a weakness, it is a powerful tool that can be used in almost any situation. The style of ballroom dances will make any Lumberjane more confident with a fresh sense of creativity, motivation and energy. The different forms of ballroom dancing not only give a great learning experience but will also show the importance of working in pairs and the ability to rely on a partner who is separate but at the same time an extension of the dancer.

To obtain the *Go Ball-istic* badge, a Lumberjanes must be able to perform one of the many dances available from start to finish with her partner. As partners, they will hold each other up and help each other if needed as they complete the dance to the best of their abilities. The lesson from this badge is something a Lumberjane will take with her for the rest of her life as she learns to understand the influence she will have on those around her. Confidence and strength is something that

Molly, we are doomed. SO DOOMED. AN UNSCALABLE MOUNTAIN OF DOOMED.

Fine?! FINE?! We are trapped here with a deeply unpleasant woman who can literally TRANSFORM INTO A BEAR, while we remain soft and small and delicious-looking...

Mal, come on, we're gonna figure this out, it's going to be fine--

...and, OH YEAH, no one knows we're here! And hey, also, additionally, there are dinosaurs!

FRIGGIN'. DINOSAURS.

Funnily enough, I don't think the dinosaurs are the weirdest thing about this place. I mean these ruins? The weird plants? "A place of lost things?" There's more to this than just a bad sci-fi novel, I think...

THOOMP

will com

The out

It help
appearan
dress f
Further
Lumber
to have
part in
Thiskv
Hardc
have
them

THIS BADGE WAS A
TOTAL PIECE OF CAKE

E UNIFORM

should be worn at camp
events when Lumberjanes
may also be worn at other
ions. It should be worn as a
the uniform dress with
rect shoes, and stocking or
ut grows her uniform or
ng ... ster Lumberjane.
a she has
her
her

The
yellow, short sl
emb
the w
choose
slacks,
made o
out-of-dc
green bere
the colla
Shoes ma
heels, roun
socks shou
the uniform. Ne...es, bracelets, o
belong with a Lumberjane unifo

KEVIN BACON WISHES HE
COULD DANCE LIKE BUBBLES

HOW TO WEAR

To look well in a uniform
uniform be kept in good c
pressed. See that the skirt is the rig
height and build, that the belt is adjus
that your shoes and stockings are in keeping with the
uniform, that you watch your posture and carry yourself
with dignity and grace. If the beret is removed indoors,
be sure that your hair is neat and kept in place with an
insonspicuous clip or ribbon. When you wear a
Lumberjane uniform you are identified as a member of
this organization and you should be doubly careful to
conduct yourself in a way that will show everyone that
courtesy and thoughtfullness are part of being a
Lumberjane. People are likely to judge a whole nation by
the selfishness of a few individuals, to criticize a whole
family because of the misconduct of one member, and to
feel unkindly toward and organization because of the

The unifor
helps to cre
in a group.
active life th
another bond
future, and pr
in order to b
Lumberjane pr
Penniquiqul Thi
Types, but m...s will wish to have one. They
can either b...e uniform, or make it themselves from
materials available at the trading post.

THIS IS TOTALLY
UN-BEAR-ABLE!

LUMBERJANES FIELD MANUAL

CHAPTER TWELVE

Lumberjanes "Arts and Crafts" Program Field

OLDIE BUT GOODIE BADGE

"Helping history stay alive."

Every year we grow older and mature as women. Like any well rounded Lumberjane, we will understand that the experiences of those older than ourselves are meant to help guide us on our path. They are the ropes on the walkway of our journey, hinting at directions that should be taken while not forcing us to stay on just one path. Being a Lumberjane is more than learning skills for the great outdoors, it is also a chance to learn from this community of unique individuals. 'Respect your elders' is not a term that is taken lightly at Lumberjane camp and it never will be. All women learn from the follies of their youth, just as each young woman could learn a different lesson from the same problem it is up to all the Lumberjanes to seek guidance in their counselors, their peers, and their elders.

The importance of the *Oldie But Goodie* badge is that it teaches respect, and how to value all the lives around

you, even if they don't visibly affect your own. We are all connected under the same sky and one decision from a young scout fifty years in the past can still affect the decisions of young Lumberjanes attending camp this day. History is important, it is a chance for us to learn from the actions of others, to see the courses that were already taken and to take a step in an all-new direction. Even our own personal histories are used as guides in every decision we make as we continue on our personal journeys.

To obtain the *Oldie But Goodie* badge a Lumberjane must help an elder in the camp. In this performance they will be able to see what is needed to assist and will do all that they can to make sure that they are able to help. They are not required to perform on their own as to be a Lumberjane means to be constantly surrounded by friends, and in this badge, all who help out will each earn their own *Oldie But Goodie* badge. It is

'Bout time you two showed up! If I had to sit here like...like... LIKE A COMMON OLD LADY and braid another rope by myself, you gals mighta been a bear's dinner tonight.

Ahhh B-Dubbs, always such a delight, it's a shame that our uncomfortably close time together is coming to a blessed end.

All right all right! Cut the sass, what's the rest of the plan, you little troublemaker?

Yeah Mal, what's the sitch?

will co...

The ...
It help...
appearan...
dress f...
Further ...
Lumber...
to have ...
part in ...
Thiskw... ...out grows her uniform or
Hardc... ...ter Lumberjane.
have ... ...ia she has
them ... ...her
...her

HOLY ANNE BANCROFT!

The ...
yellow, short sle...
emb...
the w...
choose...
slacks, ...
made o...
out-of-do...
green bere...
the colla...
Shoes may ...
heels, roun... ...ngs or
socks should ... ...th the shoes or wi...
the uniform. Ne... ...es, bracelets, or other jewelry do ...
belong with a Lumberjane uniform.

IT'S A TRAP!

HOW TO WEAR

To look well in a unifo...
uniform be kept in g...
pressed. See that the skir...
height and build, that the ...
that your shoes and stock...
uniform, that you watch your p...
with dignity and grace. If the beret is ... ...oors,
be sure that your hair is neat and kept in place with an
insonspicuous clip or ribbon. When you wear a
Lumberjane uniform you are identified as a member of
this organization and you should be doubly careful to
conduct yourself in a way that will show everyone that
courtesy and thoughtfullness are part of being a
Lumberjane. People are likely to judge a whole nation by
the selfishness of a few individuals, to criticize a whole
family because of the misconduct of one member, and to
feel unkindly toward and organization because of the

The unifo...
helps to cre...
in a group. ...
active life th...
another bond...
future, and pr...
in order to b...
Lumberjane pr...
Penniquiqul Thi... ...ore Lady
Types, but m... ...es will wish to have one. They
can either b... ...e uniform, or make it themselves from
materials available at the trading post.

MORE GLITTER!

QUIET TIME TOGETHER IN THE WOODS

THEY TRIED TO OUT FOX US

The Lumberjane uniform sh...
...neetings

...or make it ...able at the trading post.

...tivities. The ... is a
...right red neckerchief is w... ...neath
...uld be tied in a simple friendship knot.
...er black or brown and should have flat
...and a straight inner line. Stockings or
...nd in color with the shoes or with
...ces, bracelets, or other jewelry do not
...erjane uniform.

...WEAR THE UNIFORM

...orm demans first of all that the
...od condition—clean and well
...t is the right length for your own
...e belt is adjusted to your waist,
...kings are in keeping with the
...our posture and carry yourself
...gnity and grace. If the beret is removed indoors,
...e sure that your hair is neat and kept in place with an
insonspicuous clip or ribbon. When you wear a
Lumberjane uniform you are identified as a member of
this organization and you should be doubly careful to
conduct yourself in a way that will show everyone that
courtesy and thoughtfullness are part of being a
Lumberjane. People are likely to judge a whole nation by
the selfishness of a few individuals, to criticize a whole
family because of the misconduct of one member, and to
feel unkindly toward and organization because of the

The
helps
in a g
active
another
future
in or
Lumberjane p
Penniquiqul Thistle Cr...
Types, but most Lumberjanes wi...
can either buy the uniform, or make it them...
materials available at the trading post.

RIPLEY IS TOAD-ALLY AWESOME!

COVER GALLERY

Lumberjanes "Out-of-Doors" Program Field

GRUNGEON MASTER BADGE

"Put a pin in it."

There can only be one. Not really, but one day there might be a class where that is the case and it's important to remain vigilant as the lessons taught at this camp adapt and evolve with the times. At camp there will be many obstacles and challenges that the Lumberjanes will face as a team and just as many that they will face on their own. Grunge does not represent the ultimate movement within rock'n roll as every Lumberjane will learn, it is however, it was a great movement of music. Grunge was the last sort of unifying force that brought together a generation and it brought together a variety of people and creatures from any gender, age, or race. It was passionate, exciting, and those are just some of the qualities that we feel it is important for a Lumberjane to understand.

In the practice for the *Grungeon Master* badge, a Lumberjane understand what it means to go underground,

the importance of finding something that will separate her from her peers but will at the same time offer unifying aspect that will show her fellow scouts that while every member of this camp is unique and different, we are also all united in our differences. She will bring out the best of everyone she works with and will strive to bring out the best in herself as well.

To obtain the *Grungeon Master* badge, the Lumberjanes must display their knowledge in the art of plaid. They must be able to look at their challenge and understand where to place a pin and a patch. They must be able to understand what they are capable of and how their actions will affect those around them. This badge is meant to both unify the camp and help each scout show off their uniqueness and their independence. Every creature in this plane must enjoy what makes them different, embrace what separates them from the

Issue Nine Variant
MING DOYLE

Issue Twelve
CAROLYN NOWAK